Nuptse & Lhotse Go to ICELAND

Jocey Asnong

Jocey Asnong

RMB

Nuptse and Lhotse's adventures in the 'Land of Ice and Fire' were inspired by Icelanders' love of storytelling and an actual eruption. In August of 2014, Bárðarbunga, a volcano system in the heart of Iceland, woke up. For the next six months, hot magma spewed out of a fissure in the Earth, making the Holuhraun (or Nornahraun) lava fields gigantic. There are rumours that Katla Volcano is ready to wake up next.
Nuptse (Nup-see) and Lhotse (Low-zee) would like to thank all of their amazing fans from around the world. Your support and enthusiasm over the years for these globe-trotting cats has filled my heart. Special thanks goes out to Conor B., Franka S., Smári, Katie and Ollie for their help and advice when I was making this book. Thank you!!
Puffin Colony
West Fjords
SAUÐKIND OVIS ARIES
ÍSLAND 300
Snaefellsnes
ICELAND
Langjökull Glacier
REYKJAVIK
FIRST DAY
31 III 54
ISSUE
ÚTGÁFUDAGUR
Geysir
5 AURAR
ÍSLAND
Hekla Volcano

Nordur
Vestur
Austur
Suður
Krafla Volcano
Askja Volcano
Lake Mývatn
Turf Houses
Holuhraun Eruption
Hofsjökull Glacier
Bárðarbunga Volcano
Vatnajökull Glacier
Iceberg Lagoon
Laki Craters
Grímsvötn Volcano
ISLAND 500
ISLAND 6.50
DEDICATED TO
DELEVAN MORGAN,
MY 'GOBI GIRL'
May your life always be filled with adventures, stories and a love for faraway places.

Once upon a time, close to over there and not very far from here, there lived two world-famous travelling cats.

NUPTSE THE CURIOUS

Named after Mount Nuptse, a beautiful mountain near Mount Everest.

Loves her teddy bear, sweets, and her big-brother cat, Lhotse.

A scaredy cat that is sometimes brave.

LHOTSE THE COURAGEOUS
Named after Mount Lhotse, a gigantic mountain near Mount Everest.
Loves grizzly bears, books, stamps, and his little-sister cat, Nuptse.
A smarty-pants that is sometimes scared.
AVIATION
VOLUME
AGRICULTURE
Aesop's Fables
ALEXANDRIA
MATHEMATICS
BIRDS: NATURE STUDY
HORSE
Animals of Africa
SPACE TRAVEL
COOKING
MUSK-OX
INSECTS
EMBRYOLOGY
UNIVERSE
POTTERY AND PORCELAIN
DOG
TOYS
JUST ADD WATER
NAVIGATION: SHIP'S LOG
MAPS AND GLOBES
FOLKTALES
FLAGS
SHELLS
HISTORY
Fish to Glaciers
ARCTIC REGIONS: POLAR EXPLORATION
SHELTER

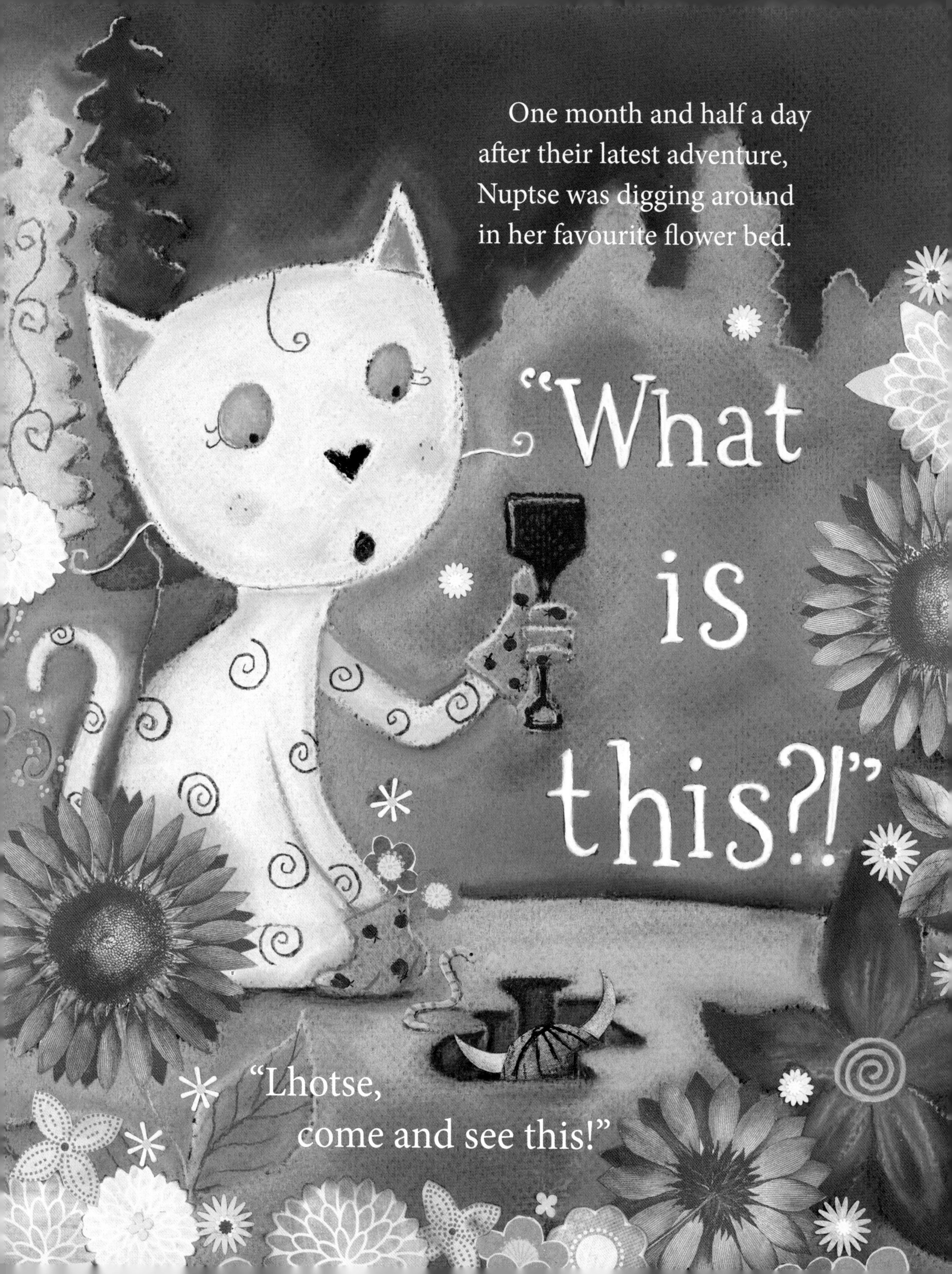

One month and half a day after their latest adventure, Nuptse was digging around in her favourite flower bed.

"What is this?!"

"Lhotse, come and see this!"

Nuptse gently placed the amazing thing she had found on top of her head.

"I can hear the sound of the sea!" she said.

"This could be an ancient Viking helmet," suggested Lhotse. "The Vikings may have been the first explorers to visit North America. Maybe they were here! We need to go to the Land of Ice to see if we can find out more about this helmet."

"But how will we get there?" asked Nuptse.

"We'll travel like Vikings and use a long ship," replied Lhotse.

"But Lhotse, we don't have a long ship," said Nuptse.

"Yes we do," said Lhotse. "Look what I found in the library!"

The cats sailed together over high seas and through fierce storms.

"A wave as tall as Mount Everest is coming right towards our boat!" whimpered Nuptse.

"Did you know that Vikings were very brave and very adventurous and sailed all over the world through storms like this?!" yelled Lhotse.

"Hang On!"

DEFINITION OF SEASICKNESS:
To get tossed around in a tiny tiny tiny tiny boat in a big big big big big ocean until you turn every colour of green.

Their ship went up and over the giant wave and came to rest on a distant shore.

"Welcome to the Land of Ice! I am Breida the Puffin Greeter."

"Are you kidding?" giggled Nuptse. "There is no ice here!"

"When Vikings discovered this island they saw how beautiful it was. They decided to keep it a secret and named it Iceland so that no one else would ever want to come here," chirped Breida.

"That is so sneaky!" laughed Lhotse.

AUK
AUK
AUK
AUK
AUK
AUK
AUK
AUK
AUK
AUK
AUK
AUK

“Is that what I think it is?” gasped Breida. She hopped over and looked at Nuptse’s helmet.

“There is something written on these horns! You must go visit Lopi the Sweatermaker. She can read patterns and she’ll know what these letters are!”

“Go all the way West until you reach the Snaefell Sea Arch. Lopi lives in a field of wool right above it.”

"I am Lopi the Sweatermaker of Lopapeysa. How may I help you?"

"Can you read what this says?" asked Lhotse. Lopi squinted at the horns. Nuptse stared at all the sweaters.

"I can only read the first letter, it's the letter K."

"The next letter is in Norse, which means we need to find an Icelandic Horse of the North. Let's go."

Lopi and the cats followed a road from West to North and through a hole in the mountains. At a meadow where the clouds fell into the sea, a small but stocky horse came running at a flying pace towards them.

"I am Thorse the Galloper. I haven't had a visitor forever and I am so excited and is that a Viking helmet and did you know that the second letter on here is a Neigh…"

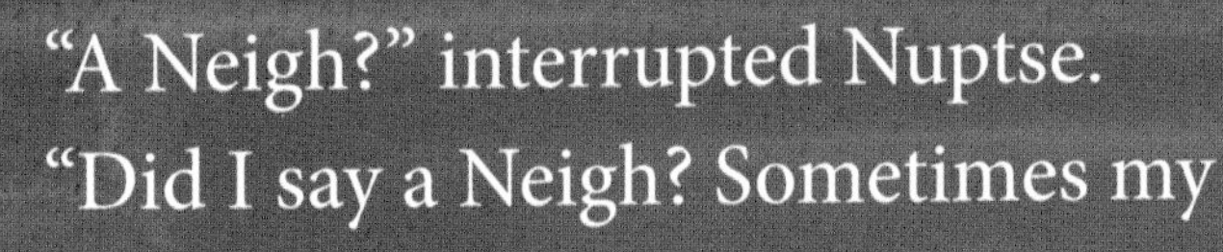

"A Neigh?" interrupted Nuptse.

"Did I say a Neigh? Sometimes my words come out at all at once and it sounds like a Neigh but what I *meant* to say is an A."

"What is the next letter?" asked Lhotse.

"I can't read it but I know a fox who can and we need to go right away and I can help and we can all be best friends!"

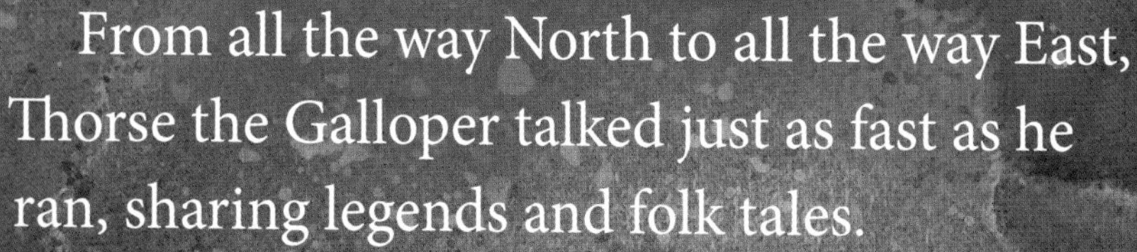

From all the way North to all the way East, Thorse the Galloper talked just as fast as he ran, sharing legends and folk tales.

“Icelandic horses are special because we know how to running walk and flying pace. All the other horses in the world forgot how.”

“We have to cross these lands on tiptoes so we don’t hurt the mossy lichen or wake up any trolls.”

“If a troll sees the sun he will surely turn to stone.”

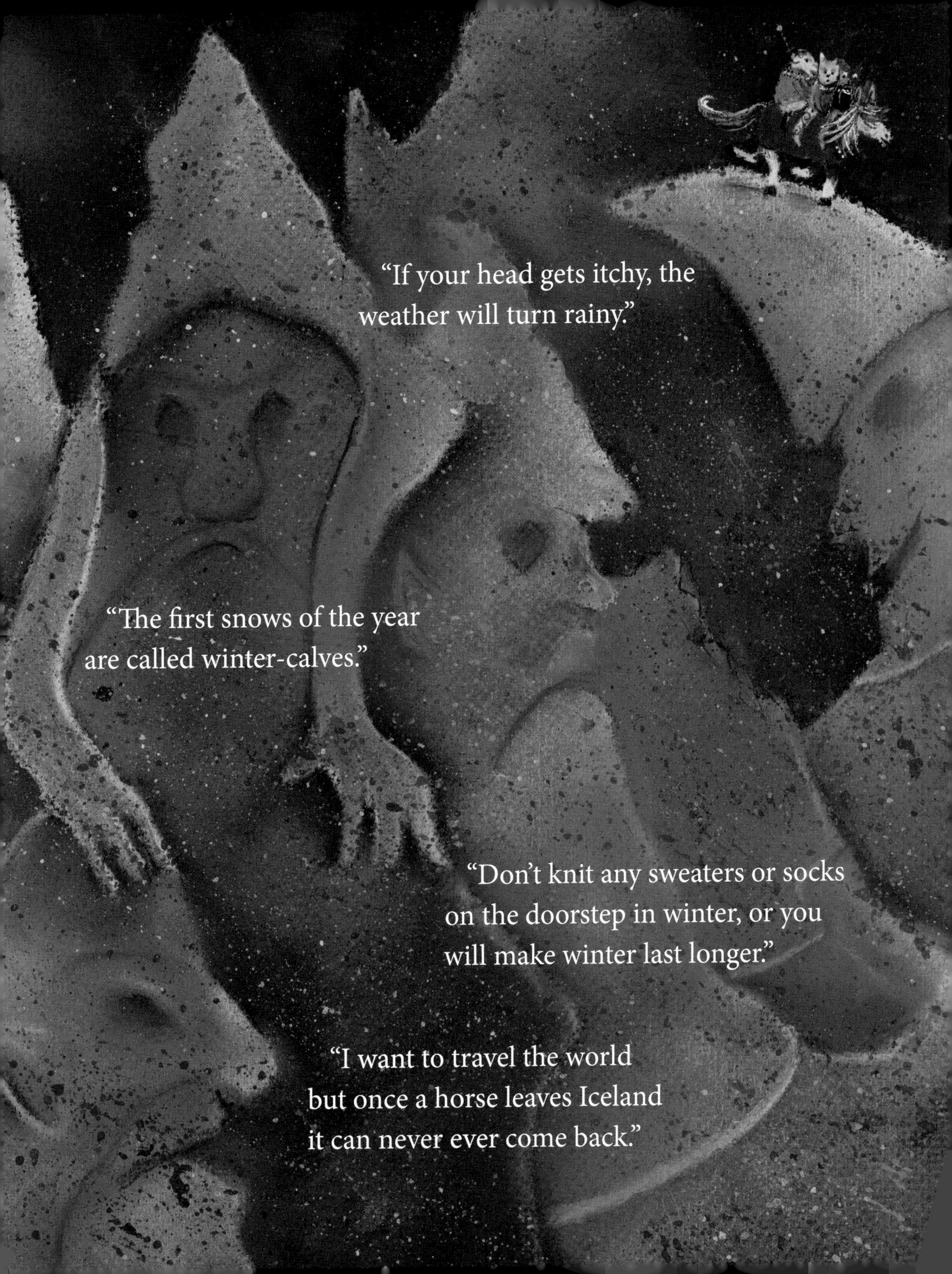

"If your head gets itchy, the
weather will turn rainy."

"The first snows of the year
are called winter-calves."

"Don't knit any sweaters or socks
on the doorstep in winter, or you
will make winter last longer."

"I want to travel the world
but once a horse leaves Iceland
it can never ever come back."

"What is that strange smell?" sniffed Lhotse,
"It stinks like rotten eggs."
"I think ....those reindeer...... are farting!"
coughed Nuptse.

"You're almost right! It is gas but it's not from the reindeer!" laughed Lopi.

"The Earth's crust looks like a giant jigsaw puzzle covering the planet but the pieces under Iceland don't match up," explained Thorse. "When the pieces get rubbed together or if they come apart, lava, magma and sulfur gas from the middle of the planet spews out."

“This is the farm of Fjórds-dottir the Arctic Fox,” announced Thorse.

“But there is nothing here,” pointed out Lhotse.

"What is all that racket out there?" called a voice from below them. "Get down off my roof before you break a hoof, and join me for dinner!"

All the THINGS that
VIKINGS and SETTLERS
Likely Ate
Dulse Sea Algae and Moss
Seabird Eggs
Dried Fish and Shark Hákarl
Fish Soup
Sheep Skyr (Yoghurt)
Berries
Barley Flour Bread
All the THINGS that
VIKINGS AND SETTLERS
Never Ate
Peanut Butter and
Jelly Sandwich
Spaghetti with
Meatballs
Hot Dogs
Ice Cream
Sundae
Pepperoni Pizza
Cheeseburger
FRIES
Chicken Nuggets
Jellybeans

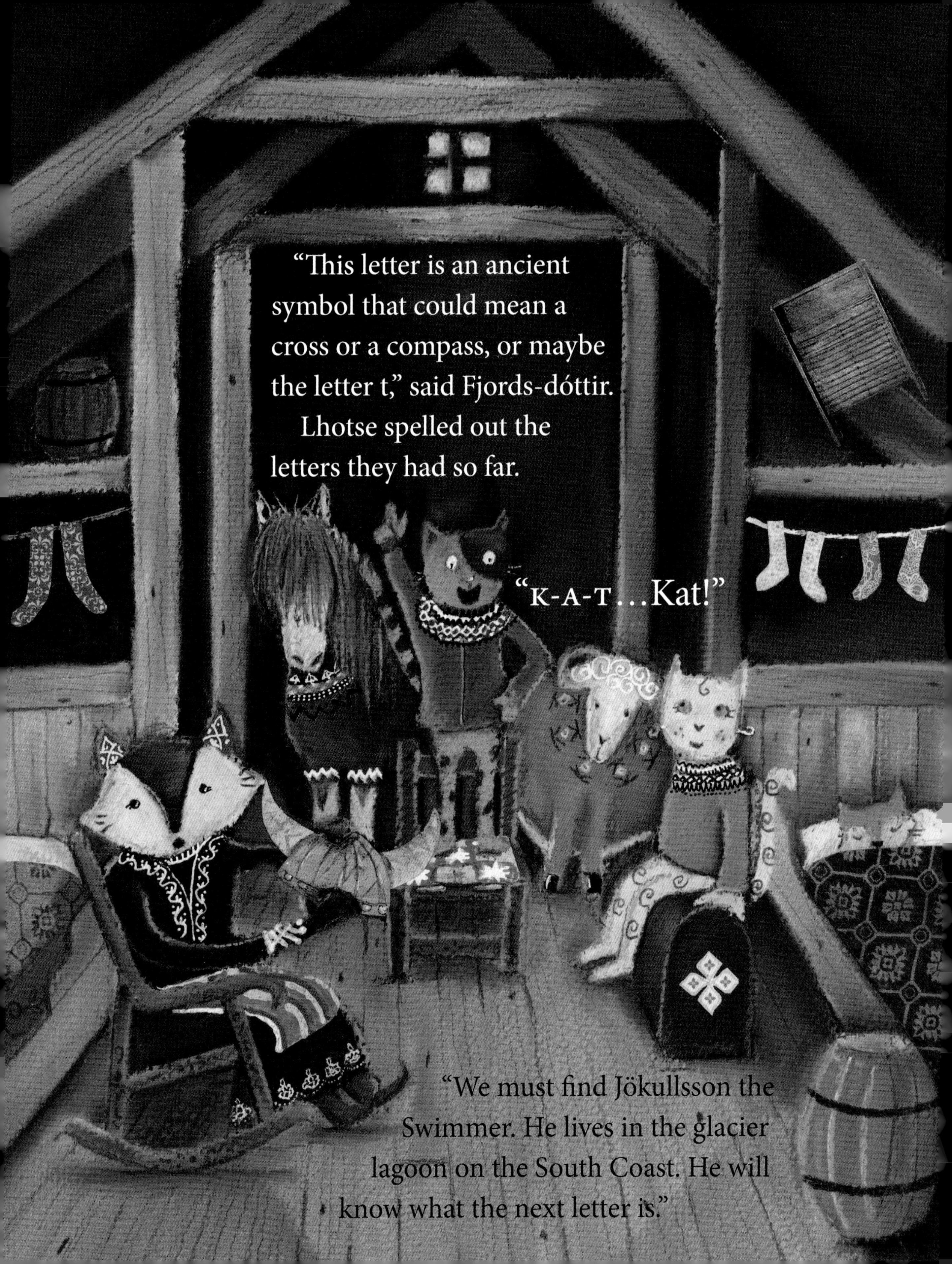

"This letter is an ancient symbol that could mean a cross or a compass, or maybe the letter t," said Fjords-dóttir.

Lhotse spelled out the letters they had so far.

"K-A-T . . . Kat!"

"We must find Jökullsson the Swimmer. He lives in the glacier lagoon on the South Coast. He will know what the next letter is."

The morning after a night that never became dark, they travelled together from the most Easterly East towards the Southernmost South.

"There are so many icebergs here!" said Nuptse. A **gigantic** seal swam towards them.

"Are you Jökullsson the Swimmer?" asked Lhotse.

"I am, but in Seal Tongue it sounds like Yökullsson," he grunted. "Now what on earth is Iceberg Blue Eyes here wearing?"

"We think it's a Viking helmet. Do you know what these letters are?" asked Nuptse.

“This is the letter L,” he paused, “but the last symbol is in the Elfish Alphabet. You’ll need to find the Hidden People to help you read it. Follow the black sand beach past the ice diamonds until you reach Seljalandsfoss. Climb the stairs behind the waterfall up into the highlands and you will find their hiding lands.”

"I found the stairs!"
said Thorse triumphantly.

They climbed up the slippery staircase behind the waterfall into the strangest land they had ever seen. They wandered through hills and high places for hours upon hours.

"This is going to be impossible!" whined Thorse. "We still don't know where your helmet came from, we are trying to find hidden people that can't be found, and now we are lost in a forest of fungus."

"This isn't impossible, we just need to think," said Lhotse.

"YOU ALMOST SAT ON TOP OF ME!" squeaked a tiny voice. An elfish girl was stomping furiously on Nuptse's tail.

"Ouch!" roared Nuptse. "I found one of the hidden people! Can you please stop doing that and tell us what this letter is?"

The girl ran up Nuptse, from tail to nose to whisker tips.

"My name is Gimli the Little, and that's either the Elfish letter for A, or it's the Huldufolk warning for an erupting volcano! What are these other letters?" she asked.

"K-A-T-L-A," spelled Fjords-dóttir.

"Uh-oh, this helmet belonged to Katla the Fire-Breathing Viking! She lives at the top of the volcano over there. Whenever she erupts, everything from her home is blown way up into the sky and then falls down all over the world. She's a hot mess!"

"Did you say Viking or volcano?" stammered Nuptse.

"She's BOTH! Katla is a Viking that can turn herself into a volcano!" cheered Gimli. "You need to give Katla back her helmet. Just don't let her see you or she'll throw fireballs at you."

LHOTSE'S SCIENCE FAIR PROJECT: *An Erupting Volcano*

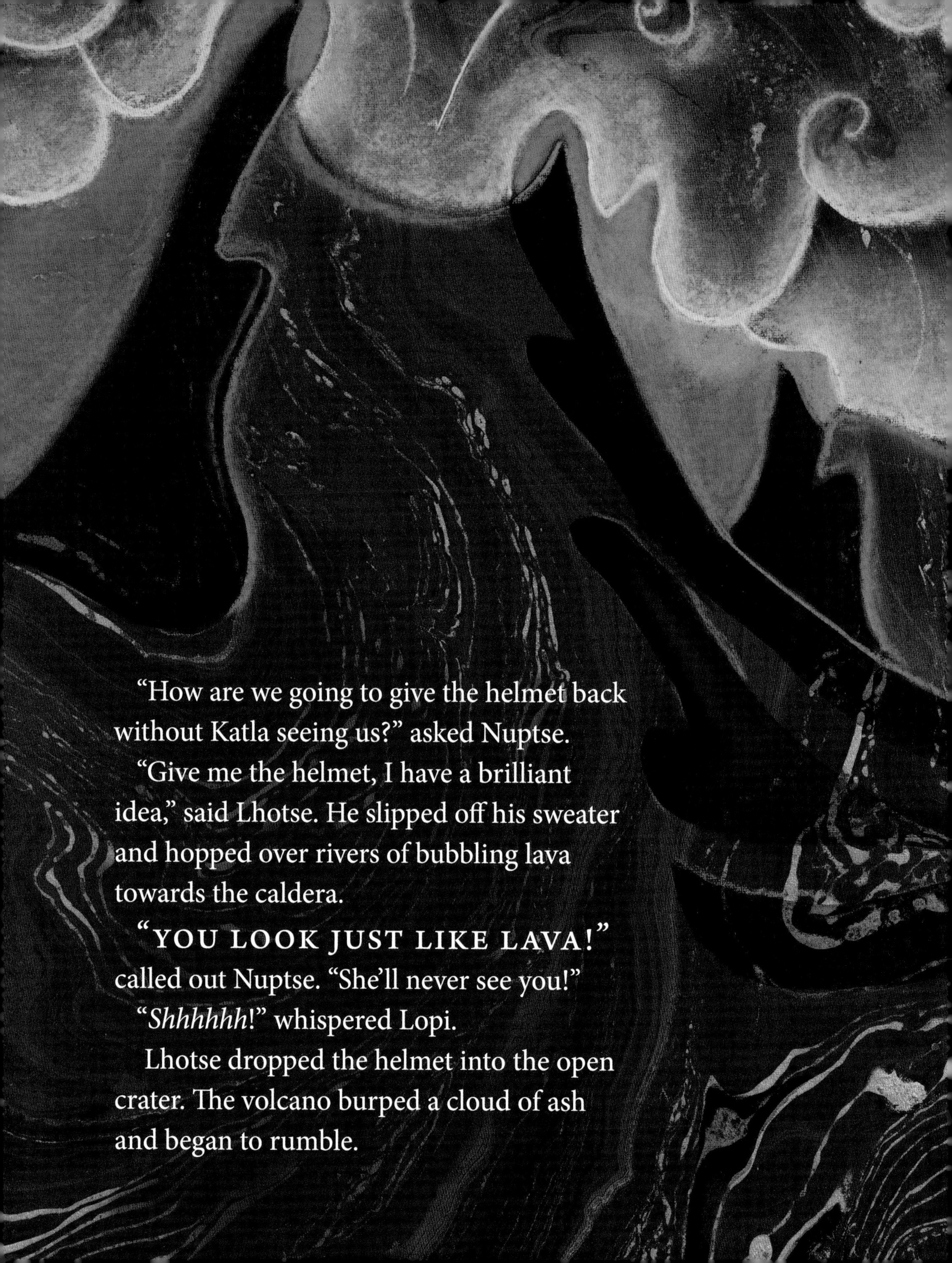

"How are we going to give the helmet back without Katla seeing us?" asked Nuptse.

"Give me the helmet, I have a brilliant idea," said Lhotse. He slipped off his sweater and hopped over rivers of bubbling lava towards the caldera.

"YOU LOOK JUST LIKE LAVA!" called out Nuptse. "She'll never see you!"

"*Shhhhhh*!" whispered Lopi.

Lhotse dropped the helmet into the open crater. The volcano burped a cloud of ash and began to rumble.

"RUN!
She's starting
to erupt!"
yelled Thorse.

"Hide in this cave I found!" directed Fjords-dóttir.

They squirmed inside the cave, slid down a slippery tunnel and splashed into an underground pool.

"It's so warm!" laughed Lhotse. "It must be heated from the volcano."

"Phew, that was a close one!" said Thorse.

"So…how do we get out of here?"

"This isn't a normal pool," Fjords-dóttir smiled,

"It's a GEYSIR!

Hang on everyone!"

"That was the best ride ever!" exclaimed Nuptse. "I think we are close to the capital city of Reykjavík now," said Lopi. "Let's celebrate with chocolate molten lava cake before we say goodbye."

The End

Whatever Happened to ...

THORSE the Galloper became the foster father for Fjords-dóttir's son 'Pup'. He is going to ask Fjords-dóttir to marry him as soon as he gets his hair cut.

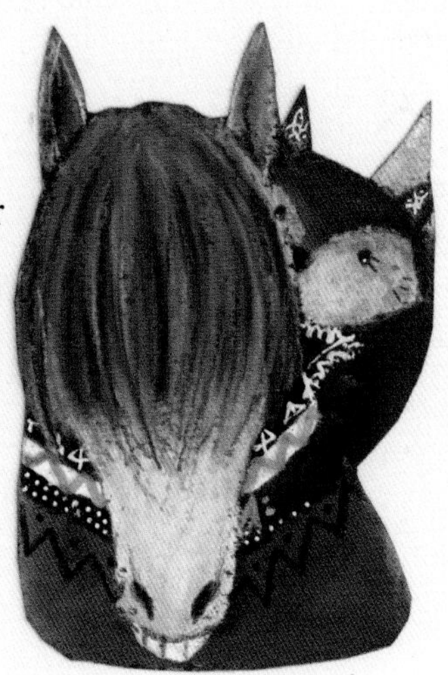

LOPI the Sweatermaker opened a Lopapeysa shop. Her bestselling sweater is the "Nuptse and Lhotse" pattern.

JÖKULLSSON the Swimmer just competed in the Winter Olympics. He won a Silver Medal in Iceberg Hurdles and Gold in the Lagoon High Dive.

FJORDS-DÓTTIR the Arctic Fox opened a farm stay guest house and restaurant. Her specialty is shark flavoured Skyr with sour cod sauce.

GIMLI HULDUFOLK moved to Gimli, Manitoba. All of her neighbours are from Iceland, but they can't see her.

BREIDA the Puffin Greeter continues to welcome new visitors to the Land of Fire and Ice.

KATLA the Fire-Breathing Viking was so happy to have her helmet back that she stopped erupting for a century and is currently working on her memoirs.

NUPTSE and LHOTSE found themselves immediately in another ridiculous adventure.